No Cookies?

By Sarah Albee

Illustrated by
Carol Nicklaus

A Random House PICTUREBACK® Book

Random House 🏠 New York

Copyright © 2001 Sesame Workshop. Sesame Street Muppets © 2001 Sesame Workshop. All rights reserved under International and Pan-American Copyright Conventions. Published in the United States by Random House, Inc., New York, and simultaneously in Canada by Random House of Canada Limited, Toronto, in conjunction with Sesame Workshop. Sesame Street, Sesame Workshop, and their logos are trademarks and service marks of Sesame Workshop.

Library of Congress Cataloging-in-Publication Data
Albee, Sarah.
No cookies? / by Sarah Albee ; illustrated by Carol Nicklaus.
p. cm. — (A Random House pictureback book)
SUMMARY: Cookie Monster's visiting nephew prefers to eat a healthy meal before enjoying a plate of freshly baked cookies.
ISBN 0-375-81334-9
[1. Cookies—Fiction. 2. Food habits—Fiction. 3. Nutrition—Fiction. 4. Monsters—Fiction. 5. Puppets—Fiction.]
I. Nicklaus, Carol, ill. II. Title. III. Random House pictureback. PZ7.A3174 No 2001 [E]—dc21 00-045901

www.randomhouse.com/kids/sesame
www.sesamestreet.com
Printed in the United States of America August 2001 10 9 8 7 6 5 4 3 2 1
PICTUREBACK, RANDOM HOUSE and colophon, and PLEASE READ TO ME and colophon are registered trademarks of Random House, Inc.

Cookie Monster's nephew Max had come for a visit. "Me so excited to have you here!" said Cookie Monster. "Me baking cookies especially for you!" He dusted the flour off his apron and beamed at the little monster.

"No cookies," said Max, shaking his furry blue head.

"Yessirree," continued Cookie Monster, who hadn't heard
what Max had said. Cookie Monster pulled the freshly baked
cookies from the oven. "Here you go, Max. Cookies finally ready!
Mmm. Help yourself. These delicious cookies, if me do say so."
    "No cookies," said Max again.

"*What* was that you said?" asked Cookie Monster, stopping in mid-bite.

"No cookies," repeated Max.

"You must be tired," said Cookie Monster. "Me put you in your stroller. We can go for a walk to get your appetite back." Cookie Monster was a little bit worried. He helped his nephew into the stroller, and out the door they went.

"Hey, Big Bird!" called Cookie Monster. "Come meet Max! Little Max is a chip off the old cookie. He just like his uncle Cookie Monster."

"Awwww. He's so cute!" said Big Bird. "I'm on my way to a picnic in the park. Why don't you two join us? There will be lots of cookies there for you and little Max."

"No cookies," said Max, clamping his mouth shut.

Big Bird looked surprised. "Gee," he said. "You did say he was *your* nephew, right?"

"Mmm-hmmm!" said Cookie Monster. He shook his head in disbelief and started pushing the stroller again.

Next, Cookie Monster and Max saw Ernie and Bert. "Hey, Cookie Monster!" Ernie called. "Bert just made some cookies! Would you and your nephew like to come inside and have some?"

Cookie Monster looked hopefully at Max, but Max just waved his arm and shook his little head.

"No cookies?" asked Cookie Monster sadly.

The little monster nodded and smiled.

Ernie and Bert looked at Max with surprise.

Soon they passed a bakery. The smell of baking cookies wafted onto the sidewalk. Cookie Monster sniffed happily. "Mmmmmmmm! COOOOOOOKIES!" he cried. "Me can't stand it! Got to have some!" Cookie Monster dashed inside with Max.

As Cookie Monster gobbled some cookies, the little monster shook his head.

"No cookies," Max said. "No cookies, no cookies, *no cookies!*"

"How could Cookie Monster's own nephew not like cookies?" mumbled Cookie Monster. "Where did me go wrong?"

Cookie Monster and Max continued on their way. "Hey, Cookie Monster!" called Baby Bear. "Look! We made cookies! Papa's were too hot and Mama's were too cool, but mine are just right! Would your nephew like to try one?"

"No cookies," said Cookie Monster faintly. "Max not feeling too good right now."

"Maybe you should take him to see the doctor!" said Elmo, who was walking by.

"Good idea!" said Cookie Monster. "Maybe he sick. That must be why he not want to eat cookies!"

At the doctor's office, Doctor Diane listened carefully to Max's chest. She looked into his eyes and then checked his ears and his throat. Finally, she pressed his tummy very gently. "Max is a very healthy little monster," she said cheerfully.

"Now *me* not feeling too good," Cookie Monster said as they left the doctor's office.

In the park, the picnic was in full swing. "Come join us, Cookie Monster!" called Zoe.

"No thanks. Max not hungry," said Cookie Monster, shaking his head sadly.

But Max was bouncing up and down in the stroller. "Num! Num! Num! Num!" he said excitedly.

"I think he wants something to eat," said Elmo. "Hey, Max! Would you like to try some of these sandwiches? And here's some salad, and some fruit and cheese and—"

"That not possible!" said Cookie Monster as he unfastened Max from his stroller.

"Nummmmmm!" shouted Max. He slid out of his stroller and raced over to the picnic table. He began eating healthy food as fast as he could.

After Max had eaten a huge, healthy lunch, he pointed to a plate of cookies. "COOOOOOOKIES!" he bellowed.

"Huh?" said Cookie Monster.

Max began gobbling the cookies.

"I guess he *was* hungry after all," Zoe commented.

"But he's a healthy little monster!" said Elmo. "He doesn't eat cookies until *after* he's eaten some food that's really good for him."

Max smiled and nodded. Then he handed his uncle a big carrot.

"He wants you to eat some healthy food, too, Cookie Monster," said Big Bird.

Cookie Monster took the carrot and gobbled it up. "Hmm. Not bad," he said. Then he ate some more vegetables. "From now on, me try to eat healthy food before me eat cookies. But now it time to go have some . . ."